Besties, and Soulmates

Stories about Pivotal Relationships

Featuring:

J.D. Blackrose
Herta B. Feely
Dakota James
Troy D. Kurz
Meredith Maslich
Joani Peacock
Jim Ryan

Edited by Terri J. Huck and Meredith Maslich

Possibilities Publishing Company

ISBN: 978-0-9861822-8-0

Published and distributed
by Possibilities Publishing Company

www.possibilitiespublishingcompany.com

Table of Contents

Editors' Note

Friendships are central to who we are. Beyond our childhood pals and later confidants, our friends can include brothers, sisters, lovers. Sometimes they seem to drop into our lives unbidden, and sometimes they have been there since the day we were born. Our attachments can form in an instant or evolve over the course of years. But true friends make life worth living.

We chose "Besties, Bromances and Soulmates" as the theme for our latest anthology because the subject is both deep and wide, and we knew we would have no trouble finding talented writers to tackle it. And we were not disappointed.

In the stories in this collection, people of all ages navigate treacherous times with the help of friends—or occasionally *because of* their loved ones. There are stories about friends who will do anything to stay together even as they struggle to understand the complex nature of friendship. And the writers of these tales have styles and viewpoints that are as diverse as friendship itself.

This is the second in a series of anthologies we have published on various topics. Check out our website (PossibilitiesPublishingCompany.com) for last year's "Trick or Treat" collection of spooky stories. And follow us on Facebook (/PossibilitiesPublishingCompany) or Twitter (@PossPubCo) to learn about upcoming anthologies.

—Terri J. Huck and Meredith Maslich
Possibilities Publishing Company

Make New Friends

Joani Peacock

I was a very lousy girl scout. In fact, I virtually flunked at being a girl scout. My uniform did not pass muster. I hated camping. I barely earned a badge.

But I do remember the song—the campfire song.

Make new friends and keep the old...

I remember a few faces and a few names lit by that firelight: Susan Sudero, Loretta Cybulski, Patty Sharlock, and the troop leader—Veronica's mom.

Tuesday afternoons we'd gather in Mrs. Lockwood's living room to munch graham crackers and braid newspapers into "sit-upons."

Susan Sudero loved SpaghettiOs, Loretta Cybulski was super smart, and Patty Sharlock was super cool. The four of us played kickball after school, and we'd stay out late, until after the sun went down. And whether by luck or providence I am not sure, these friendships made it all the way through grammar school.

So maybe I didn't flunk girl scouting after all.

Make new friends and keep the old...

In my high school days, my friends were pretty artsy-fartsy: Anne, Ricarda, and Claire. We read *Siddhartha* by Hermann Hesse, hung out at The Potters' House, watched foreign films, and listened to folk music. I learned to drink coffee and smoked my first joint. (I didn't inhale, of course!)

In college, my best friend was the boy next door—William—the best friend I was married to for 28 years. Two nerdy hippies, we loved to read, we loved the beach, and we loved our three children into adulthood. Three rocking adults I now count also as my best of friends.

Close encounters of the friendly kind are incredibly dear.

In my Montessori training days, I met Nancy, so funny and down to earth. For lunch we'd smuggle homemade sandwiches into the corner drug store, buy a Coke, and talk and talk. Thirty-eight years later, we are talking still.

Partying with preschoolers one All Hallows' Eve, I met the mother of a little bumblebee named Greta. Together Terry and I have fast-forwarded through marriage, children, and divorce. Twenty-eight years later, we remain the best of friends.

Lunch tabling at seminary in September of 1991, this recovering Catholic met a steel magnolia named Pam. After a few Thursday evening soirees at her house and a few misadventures on the road, we aptly christened ourselves Ethel and Lucy. Or was it Thelma and Louise? Doesn't matter. Twenty-four years later, we're still raising hell.

And then there is my colleague Neal. Solving unholy mysteries of an *X-Files* nature, this young curate and her rector (a nineties kind of guy) teamed up Scully and Mulder style. True believers, we continue to believe that "the truth is out there." Twenty-one years later, he is sure he's found it. Twenty-one years later, I'm searching for it still.

And my newest best friend is Mical. Mical doesn't believe in hell, and she loves to eat (a winning combination!). Under the guise of work, God brought us together three years ago. So much more than work, we've shared a whole lot of laughter, quite a few meals, and our darkest of secrets.

Make new friends and keep the old. One is silver and the other's gold.

There is alchemy going on here. The secret of the philosopher's stone is at work. And according to the philosopher Theodore Zeldin, the magic word is "curiosity." His recently published book *The Hidden Pleasures of Life* is a "curious book by a curious man," according to a review in the Times Literary Supplement by Anil Gomes.

Zeldin is possessed of an insatiable curiosity to know as many "others" as he can. His book introduces us to twenty-eight.

> "...not impersonally as falling under this or that system or category, nor superficially.... No, the point of living is to know the other properly...sharing our private thoughts and conversing on things which shape our lives.
>
> "Such curiosity demands that we give up on the superficial frivolities that grease our everyday interactions and open instead the sacred chambers of our hearts and minds, displaying in

> Virginia Woolf's words, 'the tablets bearing sacred inscriptions, which if one can spell them out would teach one everything, but are never offered openly, never made public.'"

Better than any priest, better than any sacramental confession, better even than any trip to the therapist is that rare and wonderful conversation with a "particular friend."

You lay your soul bare, and there is no judgment, no reservation, only love. Over pie, over coffee, in a restaurant, or behind closed doors, two shared souls meet. Like David and Jonathan, you get to know one another almost biblically, so to speak.

It's a gift best described by Saint Aelred of Rievaulx seven centuries ago:

> "You and I are here and I hope that Christ is between us as a third. Now no one is present to disturb our peace or to interrupt our friendly conversation. No voice, no noise invades our pleasant retreat. Yes, most beloved, open your heart now and pour whatever you please into the ears of a friend. Gratefully let us welcome the peace, the time, and the leisure."

Yes, Aelred of Rievaulx, I believe that is so.

Make new friends and keep the old. One is silver and the other's gold.

This essay previously appeared on the author's blog, "Unorthodox and Unhinged: Tales of a Manic Christian."

My Vengeful Heart

J.D. Blackrose

The thin layer of dirt shifted in the dusk. The Red Regiment shot fifty people, including women and children, and while the regiment was generally good at its job, the soldiers were drunk and instead of a volley of dead-center killing shots, they wounded many of the victims, dropping them in the pit still alive. Those dead and breathing were covered by a hastily created layer of soil. Blood bubbled up like hot tar to the surface.

A hand reached up through the earth, grasping for purchase, seeking any small mote of humanity. A soldier glanced down, took a drag on his cigarette, and smiling at his comrades, drove his thick-soled boot onto the hand, grinding the fingers into dust. Angor heard the bones crack, the scream of pain through the blood-covered mud, and the sudden silence that followed. The soldiers glared at the crowd and motioned for them to dissipate.

But Angor snuck back to the site after it was all over and watched the earth move. He and the other Dredo tribe members had stood and observed while their Unga neighbors were slaughtered. None of the Dredo said a word. They weren't Unga, and if the Red Regiment wanted to kill people, they should kill the other tribe, not theirs. They thought silence brought safety.

The dirt and sand shifted for three days before it finally stilled. Angor watched it every night at dusk, when he could get away from the fields, and wondered who was still moving. Who, of his neighbors and his friends, were scraping at the layered bodies with bloody nails, pushing up from beneath the surface, gasping for breath, swallowing dirt down their raw, parched throats?

He wondered what happened to Uzie, his best friend since childhood, who had stood with his mother, holding her hand, pretending to be a man at age fifteen, who had simply stared straight ahead and waited for the bullets. Was he one of those buried alive? Or was he dead, hand still in his mother's?

"Dad," Angor asked one week after the massacre, "what will happen to their homes and their belongings?"

"Shhh, Angor, we don't talk about it. Things will happen as they should."

Angor felt his stomach drop, and his mind was full of static. What does that mean? Nothing was as it should be.

His feet pounded the ground as he ran out and snuck in the back door of Uzie's home.

He could still smell the bacon they had for breakfast that last morning. His stomach churned, and he breathed through his mouth to keep from vomiting. The table was cool to the touch, breakfast dishes still set out, now encrusted with dried egg yolk.

The floorboards creaked under his feet as he climbed the stairs to Uzie's room. The smell of old books assailed his nose, as well as those odors distinct to his friend—leather, fresh soil, and something specifically Uzie that he could never place.

Angor lay on Uzie's bed, the cold blankets soon warming with the heat of his body, and stared at the ceiling. Uzie's ceiling, which his friend must have looked at every night. Angor tried to imagine what his friend dreamed about when he lay like this. Then the tears came, flowing down his cheeks. He couldn't move his arms or legs, not even his head. He lay there and cried into Uzie's pillow, wishing with all his heart that his friend was back. Wishing he wasn't in the ground only a few feet away. Wincing at the memory of the guns' crack and the heavy thunk of bodies falling.

The sadness swept through him like an unending tide, and for a minute, Uzie couldn't breathe, his chest too heavy to move up and down. He thought, maybe I shall just stop breathing and fade away right here. But his lungs betrayed him, and he sucked in a long breath.

He tried his body once more, a gesture of a hand, then the arm. He noticed the books on Uzie's shelf, and that compelled him to move. His mind raced with one suddenly profound purpose: to save the books. The other village members would burn the books for heat to warm their houses or to cook over, but no one would read them. Only Angor understood their value. He gathered them in a bag, threw it over his shoulder, and crept out the door, footsteps now light so no one would hear.

The worn pages were soft as he flipped through the books, recognizing poems and short stories passed from town to town and finally written down and bound into a book. Books were expensive, but Uzie had prized them and saved any money he could to buy a new one when the bookseller came to town. The bookseller, a man named Leon, came two to three times a year, bringing books and writing paper, pens and pencils. Few would buy his wares, but Uzie did, and Angor surmised that the bookseller came specifically for Uzie, who he recognized as a kindred spirit.

It occurred to Angor that Leon was an Unga tribe member, so he most likely wouldn't be back. Angor wondered if the gentle man with the ink-stained fingers was squirming half-dead under the earth, too. What good would his books do to protect him? Nothing.

The thought left him empty, unconnected to his body, his mind floating aimlessly from one terrible thought to another. But then something happened.

His mind and body reconnected and a spark lit in his gut. It grew into rage, hot, oily, and slick, worming its way through his mind, burning like a furnace in his belly. His mother summoned him for dinner and he considered not going. He sat in a hard wooden chair at the table and glared at his parents, his face paralyzed in a scowl. The boiling hot lava of his stomach juices came up to choke him, and he pushed away from the table.

"I'm not hungry."

The rage was at the soldiers who shot peaceful people like they were cattle.

The rage was directed at the Unga tribe members for not fighting back.

The rage grew at his parents and community for standing idly by.

The rage encompassed the entire country and its Dredo-led government, unstable and hateful after winning the ugly, brutal civil war.

But he saved the worst of the rage for himself, for being complicit by virtue of being a witness who did nothing.

The rage seethed inside until it needed to come out or it would burn him up from the inside. It was all he could think about.

"Angor, please go to your father and bring him his lunch," his mother requested. "I am sure he is hungry."

He looked at her, his eyes dead, giving away nothing about his inner turmoil. "No." He walked away, leaving her staring after him.

He wandered in the fields, other working diligently around him. He sat in the dirt and mud, the wet soaking through his pants, and felt nothing.

"Angor, help us out here!"

"No."

Angor's brain buzzed with the urgency to act, to do something. His stomach roiled, and he clenched and unclenched his fists continuously, and whenever he tried to sit still, he couldn't and instead swayed back and forth with the need to move.

He found the answer in one of Uzie's smallest books.

A spell.

Angor knew it was black magic and that it would be strong because it would be fueled by his hate, but in his mind, that seemed fine, even wonderful. He read the ingredient list with care, recognizing most of them. Simple herbs, household items, easy to get. But the last ingredient, the most important one, stopped him in his tracks.

A beating human heart.

The thought of killing didn't concern him, such was his fury, but the question of who it would be troubled him. Unlike the soldiers who killed without knowing who anyone was, Angor would have to kill a person he knew intimately, probably someone he had known his whole life, or the resurrection spell wouldn't work.

But no matter, he would solve it. He was bringing Uzie back.

He spent all day in the fields mulling over the plan. His mind tumbled with possibilities. Should he kill the so-called mayor of the town? No, too hard to get alone. Should he kill the field master, a man he'd known since childhood who had used a knife to clean his nails during the shooting?

Sometimes his wrath focused on his own father, who was an elder in the village and could have done something, said something, anything. Sometimes his wrath turned to the family that had taken over Uzie's house, who threw Uzie's family's things out on the grass in a refuse pile to be burned later. Angor panted with the effort to keep from screaming when he noticed that they kept the fine dishes and two handwoven rugs. The burning tears, hot and salty, streamed down his cheeks, and he squeezed his eyes shut to stop them.

Angor's rage consumed him until a blackness fell upon him. His foul mood, angry eyes, and tense body kept everyone else at bay. He felt as if an ash cloud from the monstrous smokestacks in the distance fell from the sky and wreathed him in its soot.

But if there was ever a truth to be told, it was that blackness seeks blackness, and Angor found himself alone, his ill temper keeping all others in different parts of the fields. Until a man appeared, dark as night in black clothing, a black hat and boots, but most of all, black eyes that glittered with an anger to match Angor's own.

"You seem antsy, boy," said the Stranger. "Not at peace like others in this field."

"What is it to you?" snapped Angor.

"Nothing," shrugged the Stranger. "It is only that I feel unsettled as well and recognize the same in others. You have a tension about you that I can see and feel. I, too, feel that tension."

"What do you know about how I feel?"

"We live in challenging times. Neighbor versus neighbor. Every man for himself. Survival of the fittest. Do you feel like the fittest?"

Angor stared. "No," he whispered. "I think I'm alive by an accident of fate. It was Uzie, but it could have been me."

"Ah," said the Stranger, pacing a circle. "Now we get to the heart of it. Your friend was killed but you survived. You feel guilt."

"I feel rage."

"That too."

"Again I ask, what do you know about it?"

The Stranger bobbed his head in acknowledgment of the question. "A worthy query, I agree. What do I know about guilt and rage? What do I know about the randomness of death and the vagaries of life? What do I know about *pain*?" His voice increased in volume until the word *pain* was the sound of a falling tree, loud, cracking, and final.

Unshaken by his intensity, Angor studied the Stranger. "Well, what *do* you know?"

"I lost my family in this godforsaken civil war, you pup!" roared the Stranger. "My wife. My son. Two infant daughters, twins. Even my horse and home. Believe me, I know rage."

The Stranger checked himself, taking a deep breath. "My apologies, young man. I am still quite distraught. I didn't mean to lose my temper. My madness boils just beneath the surface, like yours, but most of the time I keep it in control." He took another breath.

"It's fine. I get it."

The Stranger nodded. "Yes, you do. I can tell."

Angor scuffed the dirt with his boot. "I have a plan."

The Stranger whirled around and pinned Angor to the earth with his gaze. "What plan?"

"I don't know you. Why would I tell you?"

"Because you recognize me in yourself. Because like is attracted to like. Because pain calls to pain and anger to anger. We are in the same boat, you and I. A part of you recognizes that." He cocked his head and said, "A plan?"

"More like an idea than a plan. The final piece I need is going to be… challenging to accomplish."

The Stranger walked around Angor in a circle, hand to chin, eyes narrowed, studying him as intently as any predator studies prey. Angor shuffled uncomfortably but stood his ground, forcing himself to meet the Stranger's gaze.

"I think you should tell me about this plan, son. I have some talent with challenging things."

"I don't understand."

"Accomplishing challenging things is simply a matter of being willing to do what other people won't. Be willing to cross any boundary, experience any pain, commit any crime. I'm a desperate man. We do desperate things, and either we are successful or we die. I haven't died yet." The last held a note of regret.

Now it was Angor's turn to study his new companion. "I think maybe you can help me."

He dropped his hoe where he stood and abandoned his basket. "Let me show you something," he said to the Stranger.

He took the Stranger to the edge of his family's homestead and told him to wait. He returned a few minutes later with a bag and the spell book. His hands trembled as he handed them to the Stranger, who accepted the book with deep reverence. It was clear that he knew what the volume was and what it contained.

The bag held the simple ingredients—the lavender, the horsehair, the string, glue, and rubber bands. Most of the ingredients for binding things together. Angor figured the lavender was for smell. Bringing a dead body to life couldn't be the most pleasant on the nose.

The Stranger sat on the ground with legs crossed, focusing on the writing.

"Whose body are you going to use?" he asked, as if reading a resurrection spell was a daily occurrence.

"My friend, Uzie, was buried there." Angor pointed. "His body is in there. It is his we will call."

"Strong, young, like you?"

"Yes, with a kind heart and a keen mind, much better than my own."

"I need to think about this plan. What is its goal? You want your friend back—is that all it is?"

"No. I want my friend back, and when this works, I want to bring the others back. I want to save everybody."

The Stranger gazed at Angor with what looked like pity. "I will meet you in the fields in three days. Three days hence is the full moon. That is a powerful time to do the spell."

"But the heart! That is the problem. I've thought about it, and as angry as I am, I am having difficulty picking a person to kill."

"Leave that to me."

"We could bring your family back, too."

The Stranger turned to leave, head low. "We'll see."

Three agonizing days passed. Angor gathered the ingredients and waited. His skin prickled on the night of the full moon as he stood in the field. The wind wafted by, cold on the tips of his ears and nose, which he knew were turning red. An owl hooted in the distance, and a cloud drifted over the moon, blocking it out and plunging the field and forest beyond into utter darkness.

Angor flinched when the Stranger's hand touched his shoulder. Even though he'd been waiting for him, the appearance of the man was startling. The Stranger's right hand was on Angor's shoulder, but his left hand was held upward out from his side. As the cloud drifted on, the moonlight reappeared and illuminated what was in the Stranger's hand.

He held a pulsing pitch of black and red, and rivulets of blood ran down the man's arm and dripped to the ground below. Angor watched one drip as it fell, slowly, slowly elongating and stretching like a hand reaching to its lover, then it splashed to the ground where it was absorbed by the cracked, dry dirt.

"Hurry, you fool! We need to keep it fresh and beating!"

"Whose heart is that?" Angor asked, backing up a pace, staring at the thing.

"No one you know! Now let's get that spell started," the Stranger hissed.

Angor snapped out of his trance. "Follow me!"

Snatching his bag of tricks in his left hand, his shovel in his right, he made a beeline for the trench where the bodies lay. He dropped to his knees, reached into the bag, and placed the components in a circle on the mass grave. He glanced at the Stranger, who was staggering a little, like he couldn't keep his balance.

"What's wrong?" Angor asked.

"I'm keeping the heart beating with my own life energy. You have to hurry."

Angor pulled the spell book out of his pocket and began to chat. The wind picked up, howling into the night. Angor thought he heard wolves howling back. The noise grew until it was whirling all around them, bringing leaves, sticks, and rocks together in a cyclone around the Stranger and Angor.

Angor continued chanting and finally screamed Uzie's name and pointed to the spot in the middle of the spell circle. "Place it there!" he yelled.

The Stranger wavered for a moment, the effort of pushing against the wind almost too much for him. He placed the heart in the center and collapsed on the ground.

The earth shivered, shuffling bones beneath to bring them to the surface. The undulating dirt rocked in a wave, and partially decomposed hands and faces broke through the surface. Worms and beetles had eaten the dead eyes, but the sockets stared accusingly at Angor. Stringy hair lay lank from the heads, flesh sloughing off, bones at painful angles. Finally, Uzie's bones emerged, the mouth still open in a scream, dirt dribbling off the tongue.

That answered the question, Angor thought. He had been alive.

Angor shoveled dirt and corpses out of the way. Uzie's decaying corpse pushed forward. He was missing several fingers, and one ear had been gnawed off. He stood, putrid flesh and fetid breath. He uttered one word with his disintegrating tongue, "Live."

"Yes, Uzie! You and I together. We will bring everybody back," said Angor, eyes glowing with the burning blazes of Hell itself.

Uzie nodded at his friend, managing a grotesque smile.

The Stranger came to his knees and watched in awe as the cadaver stepped forward, reached for the throbbing heart, and ate it in three enormous bites.

The blood coursed between the corpse's fingers and covered its mouth as it shoved the pulsating meat into its maw. Angor and the Stranger could hear the flesh squelch as rotted teeth tore in, and they smelled the tang of blood in the air. In the cyclone of magic and wind, the feeling of power was intoxicating. Angor dropped his head back in his first taste of ecstasy.

The cacophony didn't last. Uzie stilled as if testing the heart's purpose, and silence set in. His eye sockets seemed to flash red, and his mouth opened. He reached for Angor, straining forward with an outstretched hand, thrashing his head, moaning, "What? What? Wha..."

Angor reached for his friend and then shrank back in horror.

The extended hand transformed into a gigantic paw.

Uzie's mangled body whipped back and forth. His head pulsed like the heart itself as he dropped to all fours. His face sprouted a snout, and his eyes gleamed gold. A thick pelt of gray and white grew, covering Uzie's entire body.

"What is happening?" screamed Angor. He pulled the weakened Stranger up by his collar. "What did you do? Whose heart was that?"

The man cackled a manic laugh as he drunkenly freed himself from Angor's grasp. "I created something new! This wolf will help you find revenge, without any moral qualms or human frailties. I give you the perfect weapon! You are weak. You couldn't do the final deed and choose a human heart. Uzie would have had that weakness, too. Now he doesn't! He's a killer bent on only one thing—revenge. With his help, you'll get them all."

The Stranger fell to the ground chortling, holding his sides.

"But I wanted to bring them back. Bring Uzie back, bring your family back!"

"You can't do that, you ignorant pup! All you can do is avenge them."

Angor looked in horror at the world's first werewolf and observed intelligence in the glowing eyes. The wolf slavered and pawed at the ground, ready to run, his heart set on finding prey. Angor had wanted his friend back, but what he got was a perfect war machine, an instrument of death targeted on the people who had destroyed his prior life, and Angor already knew the truth. The wolf wouldn't stop if left alone.

The wolf gave him one last look and headed toward the village, loping along at an unhurried pace, knowing it had all the time in the world. He glanced back over his shoulder, challenging Angor to follow.

"Uuuuzzzieeee!" Angor screamed as he watched the grinning wolf run off.

Angor reeled around, picked up his shovel, lifted it high, and brought it down on the Stranger's head with a crushing thunk. The Stranger crawled forward a foot, but another crash to his head stopped him. The Stranger's feet twitched, and his blood flowed in rivers as Angor smashed him in the head over and over again, until nothing was left but brains, shards of bone, and blood.

Angor shoveled what was left of the body into the mass grave to join the others and said the few remaining words of the spell. The ground swallowed the bodies, drew them in deep, and smoothed the exterior so no one would know what lay beneath the surface.

Angor headed to the village, where he heard screams from Uzie's former home. He reached his house, walked past his frightened parents, and grabbed a heavy coat, a rifle, and an ax. He shoved some food into a pack, hoisted it on his back, and secured the rifle and ax over his shoulders.

He turned to his parents. "If I were you, I'd leave now."

Then Angor strode out, following his former best friend who had the intelligence of a man, the heart of a wolf, and a taste for vengeance.

Crying About It

Jim Ryan

Mickey focused on keeping his bike on track between the traffic and the ditch that ran along the road to the lake. Seth was fifty feet or so ahead, his stocky eighth-grader's body leaning to the right as he let the hill take him down the steady curve.

"Keep up back there," Seth said. "Don't ride like a wuss on that new bike."

Mickey's new bike had come from his dad, who'd dropped it off at The Blocks a few days ago for his thirteenth birthday. The bike had a bright silver coat of paint, shock absorbers, and rims that weren't bent at all. It rolled nice and smooth, taking Mickey toward a much-needed swim on that summer afternoon.

Mickey and Seth had started calling Lake Hill Apartments "The Blocks" due to the rows of bland, square buildings. Just being there seemed enough to drain people, to make them give up on any sort of excitement or dreams. By the act of leaving the complex, Mickey felt cooler, his clothes and shaggy hair flapping in the wind.

"You just worry about you," Mickey said.

The cars swept by them down the slope, and as close as the bumpers and hissing tires came, they seemed even closer.

Seth also lived at The Blocks, in a building next to Mickey's. When Mickey first moved there, he had thought Seth was an awful kid. He heard him having screaming fights with his mom, calling her names he couldn't imagine calling his own mom, and things being broken.

Just before they had left for the lake that afternoon, Mickey and his mom had their own fight, which, up until recently, would have been rare for him. He didn't want to live with her anymore. All they had in common now was Mickey's dad, and Mickey loved him while she seemed to hate him. She said she'd never let him go back to his dad's—not as long as she had anything to say about it. Mickey didn't call her any names, but he made a point of slamming the door as he left. He didn't cry either. People could use things like crying against you.

Mickey and Seth stopped for a moment to let a massive tractor-trailer truck pass, then they crossed the road into the park. It was mostly empty, being a Wednesday afternoon, but the occasional dog-walker or young couple could be seen on the winding sidewalks that followed the shoreline.

"Time to take a dip," Seth said. "I'm sweating balls over here."

He leaned his bike against the guardrail near the dock and tugged his shirt off. Mickey followed his lead, and in seconds they stripped down to their shorts and ran the length of the dock. Its wooden planks were smooth and warm under Mickey's feet. He wrapped the toes of his right foot around the outer edge of the dock before hurtling into the water.

He rolled belly-up as he sank the several feet to the bottom, opening his eyes underwater as his dad had taught him. He remembered his dad's words: The water will cover your eyes just as well as any eyelid. If his dad were here now, Mickey thought, he would tell Mickey not to fight with his mom—to go home and make things right because no matter what happened, a mother wouldn't stop loving her son. Or maybe he wouldn't say that, but Mickey wished he would and wished it could be made right. He saw the sky miles above the lake, streaked with clouds and late-day sun. On the water, there were ripples of his own dramatic leap.

He surfaced.

"Mickey Mouse, look," Seth said.

"Don't call me that, you—"

"Look," Seth said, then punched Mickey in the arm. Two girls in two-piece swimsuits, probably high-schoolers, walked slowly along the length of the dock. They were laughing, glancing at one another, before jumping feet-first into the lake, hair flying around them like splashes before they ever touched the water.

Mickey had just started liking girls earlier that year. It was shortly after he and his mom moved to The Blocks when his new friend Seth had asked him, "So how do you feel about girls?" When Mickey had shrugged and said they were all right, Seth said, "You like boys?" Mickey decided that no, he didn't like boys, and so from then on he looked at girls differently.

Jessica Wheat, who had sat near Mickey during tech class that year, offered him a mint every day, and soon he began to have dreams about her. In the dreams, she'd smile at him before turning and running off. Mickey would chase her through all kinds of places. One night, he ran after her through a field of grass as high as his chest. One night, through a circus, between the shifting legs of an elephant. Most recently, he followed her up a willow tree, gripping one rough-barked limb at a time until he reached a great height and found her standing on a branch wide enough to walk along comfortably. She had her back to him, blond hair running over her shoulders like Easter grass, and just as he reached out to touch her, he woke up to find himself staring at his bedroom ceiling, ears glowing hot.

Though he wasn't really thinking about them, Mickey realized that he was staring at the two girls, who were swimming about thirty feet away from them now. Seth was bobbing next to him, also staring.

"Hey," one of the girls said. "You boys see something you like?"

"Not sure yet," Seth said. "Why don't you come over here so I can get a better look?" He smacked his lips together into a kiss.

"Why don't you try again when your balls drop?" the second girl said. She let herself fall back into the water, raised both middle fingers, and seamlessly transitioned into a backstroke. Seth and Mickey floated while the laughing girls swam away. Mickey thought of Jessica and how happy he would be to see her when school started again and the relentless heat of the summer finally began to let up.

"They couldn't handle me," Seth said with a grin.

Mickey laughed then remembered the sore spot on his arm and punched Seth back with everything he had.

"Come here, you—" Seth lunged, but Mickey had already escaped underwater, watching Seth's hands blindly grasp for him and find nothing but seaweed and silt.

The sun was setting, and Mickey was wandering around on the shoreline with Seth, sporting a bruise on his shoulder where Seth's second punch had landed. They had found an empty beer bottle just off the shore a few weeks earlier, filled to the neck with tiny bits of stone polished by the waves. It now sat in the tree-house they had built in the woods near The Blocks. Neither of them had ever drunk a beer, but it looked cool, and they kept all its original stones inside it. Mickey had the idea that they might be able to find another bottle, or some other interesting thing, if they continued looking along the shore.

"This is all just dirt and stuff," Seth said. "We look like that weird guy who hunts for buried treasure around here, but we don't even have a metal detector."

"Got any better ideas?" Mickey said. And right as he asked this he saw the biggest fish he had ever seen. It wasn't alive. Rather, Mickey was sure it had been dead for a while. It lay on its side just a little way ahead, only an inch or so of water sloshing against its sides. The fish must have been big to begin with, but it had swollen huge in the heat. Now that the sun was setting, its scales glistened blue and green and countless other colors if you were looking for them. Its eye was a slick marble, kept wet by the mild splash of the lake. Mickey thought it was beautiful, like the rainbow-colored fish from a book he'd had as a little kid.

"Aw, that's just nasty," Seth said. He had a delighted grin on his face.

"Can you imagine catching a fish like that?" Mickey was thinking about how it would pull him into the water and he'd have to reel it in as he was dragged through the waves. Anyone looking on would have to wonder who was really in control.

But Seth didn't entertain the idea. He reached down, picked up a small pebble, and flung it at the fish, which was only about ten feet away. The stone bounced off the fish's swollen gut and plopped back down into the water. Mickey loved the way the stone bounced and picked up one of his own to toss. They went back and forth for a few minutes like this, laughing in a way that bordered on hysteria as the stones scattered here and there like popcorn.

"Your turn," Mickey said, having just scored a particularly high bounce. And right as he said *turn* a rock about the size of his head flew past him toward the fish, Seth stumbling behind it. It was a broad, flat rock—a skipping stone for giants—and when it struck the fish, its body popped with a deep *fwump*. They were both splattered with a thick red substance. Mickey felt it on his chest, his arms, his lips.

"Oh, damn," Seth said. He was laughing harder than ever.

Then the smell came. It was like nothing Mickey had ever smelled before or ever wanted to smell again. It was an explosion. All that was vile and wrong was now bursting in Mickey's nose and mouth, burning in his eyes. Mickey wasn't going to join in laughing, and he wished he could beat Seth into submission and make him stop. He quickly gave up on the idea, though, because Seth was significantly stronger than him. This is one of the things that boys must keep track of—they should always know who's stronger than them and who isn't.

They ran back to the dock, wasting no time plunging into the cool water and washing all the red spots of fish off their skin. Normally, Mickey thought of the lake water as dirty, but he let it fill his mouth and rush in between his teeth to wash out what had gotten in.

"That smell," Mickey said. "It's everywhere. I can't get rid of it."

"You know what would help?" Seth was scrubbing at his scalp with his fingertips. "Crying about it."

They left the park immediately, and the bike ride home was a long one. Mickey had pulled his shirt back on over his wet body, and it repeatedly got stuck and then unstuck from his sides as he pedaled. The smell seemed to follow the whole way, riding on the draft of their bikes. Soon they were coasting down the keyhole-shaped parking area of The Blocks, sliding through shadows of buildings that loomed around them.

Mickey told Seth he'd probably see him tomorrow, locked up his bike, and went to his apartment. When he stepped inside, his mom was sitting at the dimly lit kitchen table, a mug of tea in one hand, a book in the other.

"Hi, Mom," Mickey said quietly as he started to walk past her. He was sure she would comment on the smell.

"Shoes," she said, pointing down at his damp sneakers.

Mickey kicked them off and left them on the mat. "Don't you smell that?" he said.

"Smell what?" she said, looking around as if she might see the smell he was talking about.

"Nothing," Mickey said. "Just the lake water."

In the bathroom, he dropped all his wet clothes in a heap on the linoleum and got into the shower. He washed himself with soap and scrubbed with the washcloth until his skin was raw and tender. The water steamed around him for at least a half-hour and still the smell wouldn't leave him, that awful sharp smell of fish. As the stream fell on his head and ran over his face and shut eyes, he had the thought that the only way he would escape the smell would be to leave. He had to get away from The Blocks, the lake, his mom, Seth, everything.

As he let the water run over his face, Jessica popped into his mind. Leaving The Blocks would mean leaving her as well, he realized. He remembered something his dad told him shortly after the divorce. *You're a good guy. Part of that means you're going to care a lot about people, and that will get your heart broken once in a while.*

That night, Mickey dreamed he was a fish, only he wasn't split in two on the shore. He was swimming deep in the lake with sunbeams falling like pillars around him. His scales were clean and reflected every color imaginable—blues, greens, golds—and he could swim anywhere he pleased.

Mary and Margarita

Dakota James

"Weird color," Winston grumbled. He squinted up at the sky and puffed on his cigar. "Boori," he said. "Boori!"

Boori, scratching at a piece of dirt on his wheelchair, looked up at Winston and then up at the sky. "Huh? Hey. Check out the sky."

"Must be pollution." Winston puffed on his cigar.

"Pollution? You sure?"

"Yeah," Winston grumbled as the smoke curled over his face. "Seen it in Dallas once." He scowled. "Let's go. We got a lot to do."

Winston wheeled Boori down the sidewalk, toward their townhouse and away from the cigar shop. The sick-yellow sky brooded over them, boulder-like stone-gray clouds floating toward each other like blimps of war.

"Must be a lot of pollution," Boori muttered. The only response was a noncommittal grunt from Winston.

Listening to the local news on the radio, the cigar owner howled from inside the cigar shop. *"Oo!"* The bell above the cigar shop door jingled as he rushed outside. But once outside, his eye was struck dumb by the strangeness of the sky, and he paused for a moment, forgetting why he was in such a fuss. "There was *something* I was going to tell *someone*." He scratched his chin. "What was it?" He scratched a moment more. "Ah, no matter," he said. "Was probably nothing if I don't remember."

And with that, the cigar owner stepped back into his shop.

Lipstick, eyeliner, mascara. They could do their makeup in the same mirror because of the difference in height—Boori in a wheelchair and Winston standing. They'd experimented with makeup before, but what they'd learned (if they learned anything) they'd forgotten after thirty or forty years. But since they could do their makeup together, the result wasn't too shabby. Winston had a knack for lipstick and Boori a knack for eyeliner.

Winston helped Boori wiggle into an ugly, floral print dress, then he pulled on a blouse with sunflowers on it and struggled into skintight, pale-wash jeans. They'd already slipped on the bras and stuffed them; they did this first, they told themselves, to mentally prepare for the rest of the makeover. Truth was they liked the makeup and the stuffing of the bras. It was putting on the old ugly clothes they liked less.

The last piece of the transformation was the wigs. Both wigs were the same make and color. ("It'll be less conspicuous," Winston had said. "How?" Boori had asked. "Just trust me."). Once they'd fitted the wigs over their heads, the transformation was complete. Out of the bathroom cocoon emerged two wrinkly, crinkly, disturbed-looking "women"—curly-headed and blue-haired creatures that might've been mistaken for the fraternal twins of an old queen.

"We have two minutes," Winston said. "You ready?"

"I don't know. How do I look?" Boori asked, batting his eyelashes up at Winston.

"Like a picture. Though I'm not sure *what* picture."

Incognito, the note to their families written and laid out on the coffee table in the den in plain view, the two old men—or ladies now—left their townhouse for the world beneath the strange sky.

As Winston wheeled Boori out, he asked, "What's your girl name?"

"Mary. My sister's name. What's yours?"

Winston paused to light his cigar on the porch and said, "Margarita. Now let's get out of here."

Two minutes later, there was a knock at the townhouse door. A small crowd of people—most of them in their twenties or thirties, a few of them children—were gathered on the porch. A pickup truck lurched to a stop at the curb, and a much smaller family of three stepped out onto the sidewalk. The people who were gathered around the door argued with one another in Arabic as the oldest one banged, over and over again, on the door.

"Boori!" she screeched. Screeching indeed. "It's Mary! Let us in!"

The two families exchanged greetings, and the man from the family of three approached the door. "Excuse me," he said. He turned the knob; it was unlocked.

It was silent inside. Names were called, bedroom doors were opened and closed. "Where are they?" someone asked. Mary spotted the note first and read it to herself. She screamed (in Arabic; an exclamation). The man from the family of three asked to read the note.

"It's in dad's handwriting," he said. He read it aloud.

"Dear Family—Intruders. Boori and I, as we've told you already, have no desire to be taken to this nursing home you so rudely wish to put us in. We are fine how we are despite what you think. So in the interest of preserving our right to not be sent to some godforsaken crackpot hellhole, we ain't here. We left. And we're fine. Don't go searching for us. I mean it. Just because we're old doesn't mean we're senile. Though if we ever do become senile, it will be because you all forced it upon us, damn it. Love, Grandpa Winston and Uncle Boori."

No one spoke. Winston's ten-year-old granddaughter broke the silence. "But what about the tornado?"

Everyone ran to their vehicles.

The wind stung their dolled-up faces as they cracked open the iron gate to the cemetery. Winston wheeled Boori forward and shuddered at the sight of all the tombstones.

"Why here?" he asked.

"It's peaceful. And they won't expect us to come here. You liked cemeteries once, you know. I was the one freaked out by them and freaked out by you for liking them."

"It's different when you're young," Winston said. "When you're young and immortal, it ain't weird. Different when you're old."

"Maybe you were immortal. I wasn't. I don't know. When death felt far away it was worse. Because what if it wasn't? Far away, I mean. When you know it's near and when you've seen its face—I don't know. It's peaceful."

"I've seen its face. It's a lot like yours, but less ugly."

They strolled down the pathway for a while, quiet, the strange sky above them. Then from within the cemetery— "Boori!" They flinched.

"That one of yours?" Winston asked.

"One of my nieces, I think," Boori mumbled. "Lift me out of this and put me in one of those bushes."

Bewildered, Winston stared at his friend. "What?" The voice of the girl rang out again, this time nearer. "Boori!"

"Hurry!" Boori said. "She'll recognize me. She won't recognize you—like this. All pretty and what not. C'mon."

Winston nodded and did as Boori told him. He lifted Boori, grunting, and staggered over to a thorny bush.

"Not that one!" Boori cried.

Winston staggered over to another bush, this one light green with furry leaves. But a cat yowled from within, its eyes gleaming cruelly. "*Not* that one!"

Winston, panting now, stumbled over to a dark green shrub with dark red berries. "Here you go, Goldilocks," he wheezed and set Boori down behind the shrub. "Don't eat the berries."

"Boori!" the voice rang out again, oh so near. Winston threw himself into the wheelchair. Masking his voice in a croaky falsetto (the wolf in grandma's clothing), Winston shouted, "Hello? Is someone there?"

The girl appeared from behind a humongous gravestone, an eight-foot cubic slab of weathered stone with inscriptions in cursive handwriting. She winced at the sight of the *thing* in front of her. "Hi."

"Hi."

"I'm looking for my uncle. He's in a wheelchair like yours—a *lot* like yours actually—and he's bald. Lebanese. Have you seen him? His name is Boori."

The *thing* that was Winston, smiling too broadly and eyebrows raised much too much, shook its head. Then, startled by a phony dramatic realization, the thing's lips parted. "Oh! I think I have actually! But not here. Where was it? It might've been...must've been...ah, yes! It was at the barber shop, over by the Methodist church, on the opposite side of town!"

Boori's grand-niece frowned. "Why would someone who's bald go to a barber shop?" she asked. "I'm sorry, what's your name again?"

"*Margarita*," the thing blurted. It craned its neck, pursed its cracked lips. "Hmmm. It must not have been the barber shop."

"Margarita," the grand-niece mused, elongating the vowels as if hearing the name for the first time. "Give me just a minute, Margarita. I'll be right back."

"Mmm-hmm."

The grand-niece stepped away for a moment, back behind the humongous tombstone, and pulled her cellphone out from her bra. A rustle in a nearby dark green bush made her glance over, but it was probably just a squirrel or a stray cat. She dialed a number and sighed and held the cellphone to her ear.

"Mom?" she asked. "There's a weird older lady here in the cemetery. No, it's not him. But she's in a wheelchair that's *a lot* like Uncle Boori's." She paused. "Uh-huh. Yeah, tell Grandma. It's weird. Something's weird about it." She paused again. "I don't *know*! Fine. Okay. I'll meet her at the gate. Bye."

She tapped a button on the screen to hang up and stuffed the cellphone back into her bra. Something rustled in the dark green bush again. This time it frightened her, and she gasped. "Shoo!" she said to the shrub. "Shoo!"

Margarita yawned, stretching all limbs in all directions, when the girl returned.

"You're not paralyzed?" the girl asked.

Margarita yelped (somewhere in pitch between the croaky falsetto and Winston's normal gruff baritone). "Not…entirely. It's my toes really. Can't wiggle them for nothing."

"Your toes?" the girl asked. "Tell me about that. How did that happen?"

"Shit," Boori mumbled to himself. "He has no idea, the idiot." He propped himself into an upright position and began to muddy his face, sticking twigs and dead berries in his wig, and ripped a piece of his dress, altogether making himself look ghastly.

"Twelve ingrown toenails, yes," Margarita said. "The doctors have operated on them, *sure*. But it's hopeless. They're just *so*…ingrown—"

Then the crunching of dry leaves and skinny twigs, the haggard moaning, and finally the appearance of some horrible creature dragging itself toward the girl. She screamed, screamed again.

"*Aunt Lena*! Oh my God! Oh my *God*! She's haunting me, she's finally haunting me!" The terrified girl turned and sprinted away, tripping over herself in the process.

"Hmmm," Winston said, approvingly.

Boori shifted his wig back over his head and frowned at Winston, panting. "Lena was over three hundred pounds. That's rude."

"Dying sheds the pounds," Winston offered.

The thud of a car door being slammed shut echoed through the cemetery. "Boori!" a voice screeched. The voice continued, screeching in knifelike Arabic.

"What's she saying?" Winston asked.

Boori sighed. "That if I was here and not dead yet, I would be soon because she would bury me alive." Then, "and that I don't love her."

Winston hoisted Boori back into the wheelchair.

Tornado sirens droned on and on. Winston sneezed, and rising dust clouded the crypt. He sneezed again. Outside, the sky was now a dark, putrid green and projected upon the Earth an early, gross twilight. Inside the crypt, though, it was as dark as the bottom of a well. Winston gripped the handles of Boori's wheelchair, his hands twisting. Boori was silent.

"Is it worth it?" Winston asked. "Is it worth it to not be in a nursing home if it means we're ripped apart by a tornado?" Boori didn't respond. "Jesus, I don't think it is. This tornado *scares* me, Boori. It really does."

Winston sneezed again, and the dust scattered. "Let's go home."

Boori was silent. Then, "Okay."

Winston wheeled Boori in the direction of the dim, nightmarish green light outside. The torrent of rain came suddenly, and along with it the guttural grumbling of thunder.

Husband, wife, and daughter, a family of three, stepped into the pitch-black crypt. The rainwater dripped off their clothes onto the stone floor, trapping the dust in little puddles.

"I know it's a huge problem, the two of them missing right now," the wife said, "but this is horrible. For us. The tornado could show up any minute."

"I know," the husband said.

"We should protect *ourselves*," the wife insisted. "I mean, they could be fine, couldn't they? Who *knows* where they are?"

"And they *could* be out there, like fools," he said. "Dad *is* a fool, you know. He'd get a kick out of this, us running around, drenched and in danger because of him. He always—" the husband paused. "Why did Mary tell us to come here? There's no one here. No one." He sneezed.

"Are we going to be okay?" the daughter asked, faking a brave voice.

"Safer than we would be out there," the husband said, gesturing toward the dim, nightmare-green world outside. "Much safer."

"Should we wait it out here, then? Please?" the wife asked.

The husband thought about it. "Okay. This crypt might be safer than anything else, frankly. Solid stone. Years of being rooted into the earth." He shook his head. "Sort of like Dad."

"I'm sure he'll be fine, honey."

"Hope so."

The storm winds tore Winston's and Boori's wigs off their heads; the hairpieces whizzed behind them into dismal, rainy nothingness. And still the two trudged on. The rain had smeared their makeup, and their faces looked like a sloppy Goya imitation done in watercolors.

Winston grunted. "C'mon," he said as he muscled Boori and himself through the storm. Every now and then his eyelids would flutter in exhaustion, and he would cramp. But he could've sworn that he heard their names being bellowed over the storm winds and thunder, so he continued, relentless as the sirens.

It was Boori who was bellowing over the chaos of the storm. He couldn't hear himself. He spoke from nerves. Whenever Winston would force another step, Boori would bellow louder, and whenever Winston faltered, so did Boori's voice.

"*I didn't mean for this to happen! I didn't even know there was supposed to be a tornado! Someone should've told us! I just—I wanted everything to stay the way that it was! You know? For everything to be as it was! As it's been! I like our townhouse! Our day-to-day—*things! *To be in a nursing home—it'd be worse than dying, because you'd have to* wake up *every day!*"

Winston faltered, but this time, he didn't continue. He teetered, too exhausted, his body failing him, and then slumped onto sidewalk. Boori twisted left and right.

"Winston!" he yelled. "*Winston!*"

Muted dripping. Chirp, chirp. *Chirp*. Chirp! The same damn bird that always woke Winston. He groaned and half-heartedly tossed a pillow at the window.

The window—it was still night. Midnight maybe. Maybe later. But where were the tornado sirens? Where was Boori?

Winston heard laughing from the den. The closing theme song to *I Love Lucy* played.

Winston got up from his bed and stepped into the den, groggy. He scowled at the TV. "You'll never quit this damn show, will you?"

"Nope," Boori said. "Not till I'm dead." He turned his wheelchair to face Winston. "You're alive."

"Might be." Winston plopped himself onto the loveseat and winced at the awful ache in his back. "Might not be. What happened to the tornado?"

"Missed us," Boori said. "Told you it would."

"You never said that."

"You were unconscious. I said it." Boori muted the TV. Neither spoke for a moment. "We're lucky."

"How?"

"You passed out in front of the cigar shop. Only store in town that decided a tornado wasn't worth losing business over."

"That fart's older than us, obviously." He glanced at Boori. "Did you at least get a couple more cigars?"

Boori reached beneath the pillow in his lap. Two silver-banded cigars. He gave one to Winston.

"Thanks."

They smoked, and soon the den was in a haze. Peaceful. Like the cemetery. But dusty and stale, like the crypt.

From the den, Winston and Boori heard a conversation happening outside. They turned. The voices were barely discernible.

"Do you smell that?"

"Cigars. Yeah, I smell it. That's the smell of cigar smoke."

"Those bastards are here. Are you kidding me?"

"Don't curse."

"I swear, when I get my—"

"Don't swear."

"For Christ's *sake, baby—"*

"Don't take the Lord's name in vain!"

Tiny round eyes appeared through the slits in the window blinds. Tiny round eyes suddenly at every window.

"It's the grandkids," Winston whispered. "That is *terrifying*."

There was a sweet, gentle knock at the door and then a sweet, gentle voice. "Hello? Anyone home?"

A harsher knock. "We know you're in there, Dad. Let us in."

Another knock. This one like a battering ram. And a voice screeching in knifelike Arabic.

Winston and Boori turned to each other.

"Should we?" Winston asked.

"We'll go through the back door."

Lipstick, eyeliner, mascara. They could do their makeup in the same mirror because of the difference in height, and the room in the nursing home had a fabulous full-length mirror. After three months of practicing, they'd become, well, not good but decent at the transformative process of disguising themselves.

"Just two blue-haired bitches," Margarita said, glossing her lips with lipstick. "A couple of dinosaurs in drag."

"You think it'll work this time, Margarita?"

"Absolutely. Don't have a single doubt about it."

"That's nothing new," Mary said.

"If you're unsure, let's not do this. Let's go play Scrabble with those weirdos down the hall."

"They smell like death."

"Then shut up."

Mary and Margarita finished dressing (they liked this part of it much more now, and the dresses were much prettier) and left their little room, the wigs gray but wavy and long, too. They headed down the hallway, through the dining hall, and toward the revolving doors. It was a masterful escape. And no one came searching for them. Not for a couple of hours anyway.

The Hardest Friend To Have

Troy D. Kurz

Sometimes the hardest friend to have can be the one closest to you, and for me, that friend is my brother.

It had been a while since I'd seen him, and at the time, I really didn't want to. It was several weeks after my wife's suicide when I woke alone, tired, and sick. The bed was a mess of tangled blankets, and I stirred from another night of restless sleep coated in pain. The room was dank and unclean, and the alarm rattled my ears. I rolled over to face the day, alive but not living, breathing but not feeling, my stubborn heart still beating and pushing sluggish blood through tired veins.

I sat on the edge of the bed, stomach clenched in an unforgiving knot, head still aching from lack of eating. The food I did eat only made my stomach churn worse than before. Besides, nothing tasted good since I'd become sick—sick of the world, I suppose. Sleep was what I wanted. I craved it like I had once craved sex, booze, and other devices that ensnare us in a web that's sometimes too powerful to escape.

I slid a cigarette out of a crumpled pack of cheap smokes. They might have tasted like hell and smelled like a burning trash bag, but they calmed my nerves. I lit the damned thing then dropped the lighter on the nightstand. It landed among half-empty coffee cups, beer bottles, and an overflowing ashtray. Two drags of the tobacco smoke passed my dry throat, breaking loose the night's crud in my chest. I'd come from a long line of tobacco addicts, and falling into the habit came easy to me.

It had been another night of tossed covers, turbulent twisted dreams, sweats, and long bouts of staring at the television between trips to the bathroom. I stood up, and a rush of blood went to my head. Swaying, I grabbed hold of the dresser. The noises from the house told me the kids were up, but I couldn't remember getting up to wake them. Maybe I did, maybe I didn't. The past few months were a gray, hazy blur of memories and dreams, with the real world existing on the other side of that haze.

I could hear the boys getting ready for school. The sink running in the bathroom, the toilet flushing, the refrigerator door slamming shut in the kitchen. Kids running through the house in skater shoes, crowing at each other like roosters in a barnyard. The house was small, so all the noises were right on top of you. The living room set was blaring Sponge Bob, and the dog barked from the basement at every sound.

I butted the smoke, gathered what senses I had, and peeked out the bedroom door. My youngest sat in front of the television wearing one of my old concert shirts and eating dry Froot Loops while laughing at Patrick Star. The boys suddenly caught sight of me in the doorway on their way out to the bus. I could hear the diesel engine coming down the road.

"Bye, Dad! Bye, Daddy!" they yelled on the way out. My oldest son looked at me with a worried face, the kind of face a child his age should never wear, and said, "You okay, Dad?"

"Yeah," I said, nodding my head. "You go on to school. I'll be all right," I told them, not wanting them to worry about me.

At that, he sat his cup down on the fireplace mantle then ran out the front door, left open by his younger brothers, to the big yellow bus on the hill.

Brothers—there will probably never be a stranger relationship or bond as the one between brothers, except for maybe sisters, but I wouldn't know about that. Brothers love, hate, and admire each other, and are jealous, envious, and demanding. They can play together or fight like feuding rivals, pestering, picking, and pissing one another off until blows are thrown and blood flows. They can still be friends, though, and help each other when hurt, lost, or broken.

History gives us tales of brothers who murdered their siblings for wealth and power and stories of brothers who rose together in triumph and glory. Although many a brother has died for the right to the throne, I know nothing of a royal life and never will, being a simple man. This is but a small piece of me.

Clad in sweatpants and a T-shirt, I shuffled to the door and watched the bus roll past the driveway, the boys waving through the windows. I shut the door and turned around to find a three-year-old hanging from my leg giggling, with her long dark hair brushing the floor.

"I love you, Daddy," she said, pursing her lips.

"I love you too, baby," I said. "Come on, let's get ready for Grandma."

"Okay," she said as she bounded away to her room and slung her nightclothes to the floor.

"I can dress myself," she would say if I tried to help, and so she did now, ending up in high-water jeans, a Scooby-Doo pajama shirt, and flip flops.

It had been almost two weeks since I'd been to work and a week since I'd left the house. A cloud of despair hung around me like a heavy blanket. It followed me everywhere, only lifting enough so I could perform the simplest tasks. It had grown from a worry, one single worry. As a young boy, I had spent hours wondering, waiting, and worrying. That one little innocent worry turned into a lifetime full of them, but I guess we all have to worry about something or perhaps someone. Now, though, I wish I'd never started.

I made my way to the kitchen as a slow twist started cramping my stomach, deep down inside. My legs wanted me to lie down, my head wanted me to sleep, and my stomach wanted me to either die or lose my mind trying to live. I slumped against the wall while the theme song from that damn cartoon show blared from the living room. I finally clicked the show off, and the silence was beautiful.

I turned and stared at the coffee pot. It sat cold on the counter with a thick black sludge resting in the bottom. My insides cringed at the sight.

Dear God, I just want to go back to sleep, I thought, turning back toward my bedroom. I wasn't ready for this day. Maybe tomorrow. I would have to call work again.

When I slept, all felt right. There was no sadness, no desperate aching for companionship, and no sense of loss or regret, only sleep. Quiet drifting oblivion is what I craved, the only real escape from the truths of a world gone wrong. I would lie down, stare through the television with the box fan whirring on the floor, smoke cigarettes, and drift away until the stabbing hot blades began to rip apart my bowels. I never knew when they would attack, but each time after leaving the bathroom I felt a little less alive and was glad for the bottles of Pepto-Bismol and Benadryl sitting next to the bed.

Maybe this time I'll sleep forever, I'd think. But while this was tempting,

I would always think about my children and then wish for this misery to be over so I could either rest or enjoy life with them. Although I still wondered if they'd be better off without me. That horrible thought wouldn't go away. It would come back to pester me whenever visions of a good life teasingly shone through the haze. My wife's suicide not only ended her own life but also seemed to have ended mine as well. I was in a state of survival but not quite living.

A blasting car horn cut through the clutter in my mind, letting me know Grandma was here, and the bouncing feet of my little girl told me it was time again to get up. I had to say goodbye. I followed her to the door as wrenching spasms struck me in the midsection, between my navel and groin, like a cold hand twisting my intestines into a knot. Holding my pain in and with a slight grimace, I kissed my little girl goodbye. She gave me a big hug, squeezing hard like I had taught her, then she took off out the door. I raised a lazy hand, waving to her grandma.

"You don't look so good," said Grandma, her face wrinkled and covered in makeup-hidden grief.

"I must feel like I look," I said, standing in the doorway holding my stomach. "Probably not going in today."

"You really should see a doctor," she said while buckling the car seat.

"Yeah, I know. I'll call 'em later," I said, as I had many times before, knowing the call wouldn't be made.

"All right then," she said, nodding her head. They waved goodbye, and I watched them drive away, hoping I'd see them again.

I closed the door as another twisting pain seared my stomach. The cold hand had become hot with rage. Knees bent, back slumped, hands balled into fists across my imploding guts, I made my way through the bedroom to the master bath. It seemed my life was being flushed away. My cellphone rang from where I'd knocked it to the floor, five times before going to voicemail.

Once the attack was over, I gathered what was left of myself and washed up. As my face dripped into the basin below, I caught sight of a tired, sad-looking man in the mirror and turned away. I stumbled back to bed, forgoing the phone, not calling in to work like I should, not caring, just wanting to sleep, only to sleep.

Two bennies and three cigarettes later, I had my wish, at least I think it was only two. Those were cloudy, drizzle-filled days even when the sun was shining.

The phone rang again, sounding far away, an unreal thing from some other life. In a dazed half-sleep, I crawled, almost sliding off the bed onto the floor to get it to stop. I picked it up and recognized the number. It was my brother—of all people. I couldn't believe it! I slung the phone across the room, and it broke into pieces, the battery flying into the hallway. I gritted my teeth and, in a sedative haze, began to cry.

I thought back to the day I found my wife on the kitchen floor in a comatose state from a pill she later said my brother had given her, for nerves. It put her in the hospital on a ventilator. She was covered in hoses, tape, and wires that draped over white blankets. The look she gave me when she came to, while hooked to those machines, still haunts me.

This was an accident, I had to believe, or maybe a cry for help? I don't know, but the carelessness of it hurt me.

I could only cry so much, so now I blocked them all out and burned another smoke. While dashing it out, I heard the weatherman calling for rain, rain, and more rain. Sometime that morning I fell back into darkness and dreamed of rain.

I must have left the front door unlocked because while I was floating away on a gray, windswept cloud, through dreams of darkness, I heard my name being called from the other side. It was my brother calling for me, the same brother who'd stolen from me, used me, and lied to me. If he said the sky was blue, I'd still have to look for myself. The same brother who owed me money and would ask for more, knowing he'd never be able to pay it back. I thought we had burned our bridges and the ashes had fallen away, but there he was. The last person I wanted to see was now hovering over me, shaking me from sleep and calling my name.

Memories rolled through my head like a bulldozer, tearing at the walls of sleep and my denial of life. Certain revelations had come to light after my wife's death. Things had been said and done while she was struggling with her demons that were unforgivable. Finding her with my brother in a drunken state of lust hurt me deep down inside. It's a scar I still carry. Alcohol had once again played the devil in a bottle, as it had many times before. We were no angels and had ridden with that demon more than once, but sometimes we gave him too much. Then the bulldozer in my head must have run out of fuel because everything went dark.

I awoke at the hospital frustrated and angry, the smell of alcohol, vomit, and blood in the air. He had brought me to this hellhole where endless questions assaulted my clouded mind and doctors groped and prodded at me in places no one should ever go. There was a tube in my arm, one in the back of my hand, and a menacing nurse with a catheter.

My anger grew with every poke and prod. I threatened them when they wouldn't give me a cigarette. They must have eventually drugged me. I was suddenly flooded with a warmth that rose from my stomach and spread through my body. Then sleep came, a strange colorful sleep of traveling and light. All the while I could still hear those around me, the commotion from the other side plagued by beeping machines, endless footsteps, sirens, calls from intercoms, and rolling gurneys.

"Dehydrated," I heard them say.

"Maybe food poisoning?" they mused.

"Is he on drugs or something?" someone asked while draining my blood with another sharp needle.

I was certain that I'd drift away not in my bed but here in this bright hospital of sickness, pain, and death.

Something happened as I lay in the hospital drifting through those morphine clouds. Something inside me awoke, a part of me I thought had died along with my wife. It had remained hiding inside, like a scared child. It was me. I was the scared child in a grown man's body. I looked on myself with pity and shame, forcing myself to face the truth. No matter what had happened in the past, I had to live, and to live I had to wake up.

There was a release as the despair rose from me. A writhing black mist, unformed and unholy, floated out of the room to lie upon someone else or drift away into nightmares. I watched it go as new life filled my tired body—or maybe it was the morphine?

I don't remember leaving the hospital or the ride home. Only waking up in my bed to the late-afternoon sun creeping through my bedroom window. The clutter on my nightstand was gone. The dirty clothes removed and the ashtray emptied and clean. Inside I felt warm, but it was a nice warmth unlike the wrenching pains from before. My stomach was sore but calm. I lay listening to the birds chirping in the patch of woods next to the house. The television was a black screen, cold and quiet, and I left it that way.

There was a note on the clean dresser top where once were piled newspapers, magazines, and empty pink bottles. It simply said, "I love you, brother! Now get your ass up and live! You son of a bitch!"

Reading it made me smile, it made me laugh, and it made me cry. It made me get out of bed. I took a long, hot shower, shaved, groomed, put on fresh clothes, and went for a drive.

I cruised the back roads, driving past the old house where we grew up, the elementary and high schools we attended, and the field where we won our only soccer trophy, the year he played goalie. He was a beast in front of the goal. You would think he had four arms and eight hands. One ball might have gotten by him that season, but the rest were denied.

Eventually, I ended up at the cemetery where my wife had been laid to rest. I parked near the front and went for a walk in the sunshine. I guess the weatherman had been wrong. It might rain later, but for now, I was alive and walking in the sun of the only world I had, and it was beautiful. The tears came as I visited old relatives, long dead and recently deceased—grandparents, aunts, uncles, cousins, friends, my father, and last of all my wife. While standing in front of her tomb, I sent her a kiss through the tips of my fingers into the engraved letters of her name as I traced them one last time. I said goodbye that day and prayed that doing so would let her rest as well as me. Then I turned and went home to live again.

Walking away, I couldn't help but think of my brother. Somehow he'd found out I was sick and then found the love inside to come see if his little bro was dying or just thinking about it. I believe now it was a case of both. Something attacked my system while I attacked myself, and in the end I almost died.

It can be a hard thing to love someone when you're angry with them. And when that anger turns to disgust, it can cast a darkness on you that might not lift. Today, though, I feel free of the heavy blanket that had kept me in the dark, and I remember.

I remember the crazy things my brother would do when we were young. I can still see him running up the hallway, spinning around in midair, mooning us, then farting before taking off back to the bedroom. He would be gone before my dad could swat him. We could hear him laughing as the cloud of funk rolled over us.

I remember jamming to Kiss records in our tiny bedroom, him pretending to be the Demon and me the Spaceman. We were the masters of smoking guitars, breathing fire, and spitting blood.

I also remember playing one-on-one football in the front yard. He was fast then and stronger than me. I paid hell out there on the grass, but it helped toughen me up.

I'll never forget the fish we caught on old bamboo poles, learning to shoot .22 rifles with our dad and our first concert seeing Judas Priest when we were finally old enough to drive. My brother taught me how to ride a motorcycle without killing myself, showed me how to find the best places to hunt deer, and, as we grew older, how to not get caught doing things we weren't supposed to do.

I remember the tougher times, too—the accidents from our childhood, a sprained ankle from jumping a creek, a black eye from a missed softball, stitches and road rash, the car wrecks when we were teens, and the one that almost killed him in '90.

Our teenage years were lived under a cloud of mourning and denial, sprinkled with good times and random craziness after the death of our father. We'd lost him way too early in life, young boys who'd become teenagers and didn't know how to act. We had looked up to him and counted on him, but we had lost him. We would always struggle, wondering why he'd been taken. The innocent years were over for us then, but we survived.

Since that dark time in my life, I've quit smoking, moved on with someone new, and have promised to enjoy life. My brother might be the hardest friend to have, and even though I might not like him very much at times, I'll always love him and will always remember that if not for him, I might still be asleep.

Giggles

Meredith Maslich

The silence of my small apartment is shattered by the sound of shrill, relentless giggling coming through the window above my desk. It's unmistakably the sound of an adult woman, and I'm filled with irritation as I throw down my markers. My concentration shattered, I head to the kitchen to start dinner while wondering what kind of woman giggles. Actually giggles.

I used to giggle.

The thought comes to me so unexpected and unbidden that for a moment I wonder if someone had actually spoken to me. Feeling silly but unable to resist, I glance around and confirm that the small apartment is empty.

I can definitely remember giggling...once.

I think I used to enjoy cooking, too, I think as I squish raw ground beef, eggs, and bread crumbs together. It feels like brains. Not that I would know what brains feel like, being neither a neurosurgeon nor a psycho killer, but if I had to guess, I'd say they felt similar to this. *Maybe that was when cooking was more novelty than chore.*

I think I used to even full out belly laugh sometimes...right?

I plop the gelatinous mixture into a baking dish and form it into a loaf shape. *Why a loaf? Why not a star? Or a tulip? I used to create art out of everything.* Of this much, I am positive, but I don't want to think about how long it's been since I used my hands for more than manipulating food and transporting clothes between closet and laundry room.

After shoving the baking pan and traditionally shaped loaf of meat into the oven next to the baking potatoes, I glance at the clock: 4:45.

Fifteen minutes. I can probably get the dishwasher loaded before he calls. He hates it when I'm doing something while we talk, thinks I'm not listening. Not that listening to him complain about his day requires much focus.

When did the giggling stop? Or better yet, why did it stop?

I shake myself in an effort to reset my thoughts. Surely there is something better I could be using my mind for. I pause with a lunch plate halfway to the dishwasher while I try to come up with something better to think about. The phone rings and saves me from the effort.

Glancing at the caller ID, I take a deep breath before I put the phone to my ear and say brightly, "Hi, honey!"

"Hi," comes his flat but not exactly unhappy-sounding voice. "I'm in the car."

"Great! Dinner is in the oven." When he doesn't respond, I follow up with "Meatloaf!"

"Okay," he says around a yawn. "God, I'm exhausted, this job is killing me."

This is his standard opening for the drive-home rant, which differs from his dinner rant only because it occurs while he's in the car and not at the dinner table. I pick up a sponge and begin to wipe down the clean counters.

When did I start cleaning clean counters? An image of a white countertop from many homes ago pops into my head. It's covered with coffee stains, jelly spots, and crumbs. *Was that back when I was a giggler?*

"I mean, can you believe that?"

I have no idea what Michael is referring to, and yet there is only one answer: "No. I can't. That's ridiculous."

"I know! And I told him, I said..."

I set the sponge on the edge of my sparkling sink and walk toward the laundry closet, plumping plump cushions on the way and pausing at the alcove that serves as my "studio." I switch off the desk lamp and avoid looking at the half-finished, uninspired image of hand-drawn overlapping hearts and flowers that will eventually receive a banner with an empty sentiment like "You lift me up!" before it becomes a mass-marketed greeting card. If I think too much about it, I run the risk of tearing it up or flinging paint at it in an attempt to resuscitate it.

I open the dryer and begin folding clothes and stacking them on top of the washer.

I used to leave my clothes piled on the washer and just take what I needed each morning until the pile was gone and then start over.

I fold one of Michael's T-shirts and notice my clean and even nails as my hands smooth out the wrinkles. *That was when my nails were uneven, my skin stained with paint. Back when chaos and disorder felt rebellious instead of—*

"Can you even imagine?" Again, I have no idea what Michael is referring to, and yet I respond confidently:

"No, that would just be..." I pause before offering an adjective.

"Crazy."

"Crazy!" I echo as if it had been on the tip of my tongue. I glance at the clock: 5:30. I fold the last of his T-shirts and flop it onto the pile before returning to the kitchen.

I open the freezer and pull out a bag of frozen corn. Michael won't eat anything green, something I didn't learn until after we were married.

As I pull a glass serving bowl out of the cupboards I am careful not to let it clink against the other dishes.

"Okay," he says, "I'm turning onto our street. I'll see you in a few."

"Okay, bye," I say, but he has already hung up. It took me a while to get used to this habit of his, but like so many things about Michael now, it has more to do with him than me. Except in the way that it makes me feel. But that is rarely the point anymore.

The front door swings open just as I am pulling the meatloaf out of the oven. I set it on top of the stove, slide my oven mitts off, and turn toward the door just as Michael appears, shaggy brown hair gently curling around a worn-down—though still handsome—face, tie loosened, jacket left on the chair by the front door. I arrange my face into an expression of happiness and step toward him. He leans in to kiss me as is his custom, but today, as has not been his custom for awhile, he slides his arms around my waist and pulls me to him in a warm, tight hug.

"This is the best part of my day." His voice is a whisper against my hair. "Have I ever told you that?"

Nope.

"Me, too," I say as I let myself relax into the embrace.

Too soon he pulls back, says, "Dinner smells good. I'm starved, skipped lunch today."

I watch him wander to the table and pull out his chair, then I turn my attention back to the food. I move the meatloaf onto a platter and set it on the table.

"The thing that really got me about this jack-off today was that he acted like he was doing *me* a favor, you know?" Michael says, picking up the conversation from the car.

I return to the stove and place a baked potato on each plate and set the plates on the table on my way to the microwave to get the corn, making interested noises as he continues to talk. I slice and serve the meatloaf, then scoop corn onto our plates.

College was definitely a giggling period. I can clearly remember much giggling in the studios. So it was after that…

"Everything okay?"

It takes me a minute to realize that Michael has directed a question toward me in the middle of his rant. I am momentarily mute in my surprise, but then I say, "Yes. Sure. Why?"

"Because you put the corn on my napkin."

I look down and see that his fork is bisected by yellow pebbles.

"Oh, sorry, I—"

I panic, wondering how to explain that I was distracted by thinking of the last time I was me. But with a flash of a teasing smile, he's gone back to his story.

"So he finally decides he'll take the fridge but not the stove, which doesn't do much for me since I'd offered him a discount on the fridge assuming he'd buy the stove at full price. Did I tell you how he…"

I begin my mealtime ritual of chopping up and reorganizing the food on my plate. *Maybe I'm making too much of this. Just because I can't remember the last time I giggled doesn't mean…* I shake my head to quiet my thoughts and refocus my attention on Michael just as he finishes his story.

"Well, the important thing is you made a sale, right?"

Michael shrugs as he forks a large piece of meat into his mouth, and I watch as an emaciated kernel of corn falls just before reaching his lips.

I take a deep breath. "I was reading a review of a new Indian restaurant downtown. Maybe we could try it out this weekend?" I avoid looking him in the eye, pretending that if I can't see the darkness settle in, it won't happen.

His fork stops en route to his mouth and then returns to the plate. "You know how I feel about restaurants."

"You used to love Indian food. And you've had a good couple of weeks, so I thought maybe we could just try it."

"You know I really only like your cooking now." He pauses and studies his food-laden fork for an extended moment. "Why are you always pushing me?"

So I'll know when you're movable.

"It was just an idea. Don't worry about it." I push my chair back and take my plate to the sink. And I hear his fork clank angrily against his plate as he sighs heavily. Quickly I scrape the hunks of meatloaf and corn into the disposal and plop my untouched potato into the garbage pail.

"Great. Now you're upset, and dinner—the one thing I look forward to all day—is ruined."

I refuse to process the implication that it is my food and not me that makes coming home special. *Are they really separate?*

I hear him slide his chair back and wonder what he'll do next.

"You had to push. Even though you know." His voice is equal parts accusation and childish whine.

I remain silent at the sink as he shuffles toward the living room, watching as dusk turns the world outside soft and pretty. A memory tickles the edge of my mind—another sunset, another couple, another lifetime. Our laughter rings in my ears, and my body tingles with the sensory memory of unbounded love and unadulterated optimism, which is quickly replaced with a wave of embarrassment for that naïve and oblivious girl who believed there would always be an easy reason to laugh.

The sound of the TV brings me back, and I pick up his empty plate and place it in the dishwasher. As I'm wrapping up leftovers for his lunch tomorrow, his return to the kitchen surprises me, and I continue putting food into plastic containers as I wait to see what comes next, no longer able to predict his moods or behavior.

"Look. I'm sorry about the restaurant thing." His voice is a murmur behind me.

"It's fine," I say, my voice cheerful, giving him the opportunity to believe I'm sincere.

"I'm sorry I'm not better yet."

"How do you even know, if you're never willing to try?" The words are out of my mouth before I even knew they were in my head.

He looks like I've slapped him. This isn't the script. He apologizes for lashing out, and I let him off the hook. That's the routine. The routine I helped craft. But now I've gone rogue and he doesn't know his next line.

Let it go. Get back on script.

"You're hiding out here, but why? It's not like everything is so great inside this apartment." I drop the Tupperware and spin to face him. "Are you really happy living this way?" *I'm not happy living this way.*

I watch him struggle to catch up, emotions washing over his face, and I wonder which way he'll tip: collapsing inward or exploding outward.

Get back on script. This is not your role, I tell myself. I'm in dangerous territory. But I can't. I can't hide with him anymore. I need fresh air.

He takes a deep breath, and I hold mine. He rakes his hand back and forth through his shaggy hair, and I take a step back, pressing myself against the counter. I see he's preparing to explode out, and I feel a tingle of electricity zip through me. *Finally. A sign of life.*

"Happy?" he asks, as if unsure how to pronounce it. "Happy?" he repeats, his voice soft in an unnerving way. "What does that even mean?"

He steps toward me, his arm hovering above his spiked-up hair. "I mean, I'm here. I'm alive. Isn't that enough?" His voice is deep and loud and has an undercurrent of emotion it has been missing since…before.

He takes a step back and turns away from me. His shoulders straighten, and his head tilts up, and it almost feels like moving backward in time.

"I go out to a shitty fucking job every goddamn day so I can bring home a fucking paycheck. So I can take care of you. What the fuck does 'happy' even have to do with anything?"

I watch him pacing our small white-on-beige kitchen like a caged animal, pawing at his hair like he'd just discovered it wasn't a buzz cut anymore. I plant my feet and square my shoulders, focusing on taking slow, even breaths. We've moved into uncharted territory, and it might fall on me to bring us back to base. That is my role.

He turns toward the front door, and I wonder if he's simply going to walk away. *Would that be good or bad? If he walked out and never came back, would that be easier or harder?*

His voice breaks into my thoughts.

"Because I'm the husband." The rich depth of his voice has been undercut by the rasp of repressed emotion. "I'm The Husband. The Provider. That's what I'm supposed to do. And I am the guy who does what he's supposed to do. Who does what it takes to get the job done. No matter what."

He turns to face me again, and I suspect that he's struggling between staying here and going back there. I maintain my ready pose and wait silently. Now I understand we can never move forward if we never go back.

"I went through the gates of hell," he says. "I walked straight through the fire, and I did my job. Just like everyone else in my unit. But somehow I'm the one who came back."

His eyes darken with emotion and dart from side to side. "I'm not special," he whispers. "But I guess I'm lucky, right?"

He says "lucky" as if it's a slur. Turning away from me, staring at the blank wall with the scuffed paint, he starts to yell.

"I got to come back. That's supposed to be the ultimate reward, right? I survived. I got to come *home*. I *get* to wake up every morning and go to a shitty job, which is more than any of them got. Plus as a bonus, no one gets blown up at this job, right? So obviously I'm the lucky one."

He turns and pins me with his gaze. For several minutes, the only sound is his ragged breathing, and I hold his gaze as I try to see inside this man to find the one I married.

His shoulders slump, and he shakes his head. "Happy is a fucking luxury. Happy is…I don't even know what happy is. I'm doing my job. I'm taking care of you. I'm living, and I'm doing the best I can."

His voice has softened, but he hasn't relaxed, he hasn't returned to the stooped, soft-edged stance he affected after he got home.

If he wasn't obligated to me, would he be happier?

The thought slams through me like a tidal wave, and my heart stops. This isn't a thread I want to pull on anymore. I want to go back. Back on script. Back on familiar ground.

"Michael," I reach toward him but don't touch him. "It's okay," I whisper. "We're okay."

His eyes dart left then right, his stance softens, and I watch him coming back from then and into now as he crosses his arms over his narrow chest in a self-protective stance, a mannerism he came back with. For the first time, it feels more comforting than foreign.

"I got to come home. So why is it so wrong that I don't want to leave it unless absolutely necessary?"

He whispers so softly that I wonder if I imagined it.

"I know I am lucky to have you," he says, his voice a littler clearer, his eyes searching mine. "I'm sorry that I'm all you have."

His voice catches, and I immediately move toward him, knowing the drill, propelled by a familiar mix of love and obligation. We are back on script.

"No, baby, don't say that." I wrap my arms around him and pull his face down to nestle in the curve of my neck. "Don't say that. You're my whole life."

"You should leave me," he says, not for the first time. But this time I wonder if it might be a plea instead of the empty offer I've always thought it was.

"Stop it, Michael, please." I lean back and hold his face between my hands as my eyes fill with tears. "Remember when you were deployed and we rushed out to lease this apartment so I'd be able to wait for you in a place that was ours?" He nods gently. "And remember when you were in the hospital in Germany and I refused to leave your side, and you told me you needed me to go outside so I could bring fresh air back in for you—"

"And you'd come back and draw me pictures of the grounds," he says with a faraway smile.

I nod, remembering how we were so good at taking care of each other back then. "And all those months in rehab, when I pinky-swore I wouldn't leave no matter the outcome? Why would I break those promises, give up now, when the hard part is over?"

Please let the hard part be over!

Michael nods, his sad, beautiful brown eyes holding mine. *When did his eyes become so sad? Maybe that's why I stopped giggling.* He bends to let his head rest in the curve of my neck again, and I soak in the feeling of supporting his weight as I stroke his back.

"Come watch TV with me?" he asks after a moment.

"Sure," I say, relieved to have avoided a meltdown that could have kept us both prisoner for days, then realize that this is progress and try to take heart in that knowledge. *We are not at the end of this journey yet.*

I take his hand as we walk to the couch. I sit down at one end, and he lays his head in my lap. I rest my left hand on his chest, and my fingers automatically begin to move across the hard ribbons of scars cascading from his shoulder. My right hand plays with his hair, still amused by the sensation of the soft locks slipping between my fingers.

What if I'm more in love with the idea of not quitting than with him?

The thought bubbles up from some hidden depth and terrifies me. That's when I remember: giggling as we chased each other around campus, an unlikely couple—the ROTC cadet and the artist. Then giggling through the overseas phone calls and video chats. Giggling as I sat next to his hospital bed planning our wedding, assuring him that this was just a small setback, nothing to worry about.

"Sometimes I really don't know why you're with me," he says softly, bringing me back to the present.

Because I don't know how to give up now. "Because I love you."

"But why?"

"Because—" I begin, but my voice breaks on a wave of images of a young, brash infantryman with an easy smile and a sharp wit. A brilliant, gentle, and adventurous man who made me believe I could be anything as long as he loved me.

I start again, speaking slowly as I pick through this neglected terrain of my heart. "Because you are *(were)* funny and brave. Because of your deep brown eyes and gentle hands. Because you see *(saw)* and accept*(ed)* me for who I am *(was)*. I don't *(didn't)* need to filter my thoughts or pretend I'm not *(wasn't)* a flighty, silly artist."

And then I stumble into a hidden ravine and am startled by what I find. I wait a beat before voicing it. "Because you nicknamed me Giggles instead of wanting me to be quiet. Because when you wrap your arms around me, I still feel safer than I ever have without you. And because I can't picture a life that doesn't include you."

Michael is silent for so long I wonder if he's fallen asleep. Then he says, "You don't giggle anymore."

I freeze at his words, unprepared for that observation and the opening it presents.

"Let's go to bed," I say eventually, choosing retreat.

I reach for the remote and click off the TV. In the darkness Michael stands, then reaches down for my hand and pulls me up to face him.

"Just a small setback," he whispers. His hand strokes my cheek, and his lips come to rest gently against mine. "Nothing to worry about," he breathes into me.

Choosing for now to believe, I let his familiar smell and the weight of his arms around me push all other thoughts from my mind as we walk arm in arm.

The Last Time

Herta B. Feely

The last time I saw him, in 1975, he walked through the door of the small Berkeley house I shared with two women, and my girlfriend's Doberman bit him in the knee. I thought he deserved that—at least that. He deserved worse. I also thought dogs know who's good and who's bad. They bite the bad ones.

The time before that, maybe early 1974, I saw him in his San Francisco flat, and he started screaming and hitting me, blaming me for things I hadn't done. Then he ran to the back of his apartment and I thought he was getting a gun, so I ran outside, slamming the door behind me. It opened a moment later, and I thought he might shoot me in the back, but he only threw my suitcase at me.

Collecting my leather bag had been the pretext for my visit; the real reason had been to see him—one last time, I told myself—because, after all, I'd spent three months in a Colombian prison for smuggling drugs for him, and weeks had passed since I'd returned and he'd refused to see me.

I was desperate to talk to him to find out what had happened after I last saw him leaving the customs area at the Bogotá airport. Of the four of us, he was the only one not carrying—the brains behind the operation never carries. I also hoped he might finally show a little sympathy or appreciation for my time in Buen Pastor. He hadn't sent a single note, though he had sent money. At the time, in 1973, I convinced myself that this alone meant he still cared. I clung to that belief through each endless day of waiting, through each promise that I'd be released and wasn't.

I don't remember much about the last time I saw him, except the surprise that registered on his face when the dog chomped on his knee, the sense of injustice, the pain. He was tall, lean, and handsome. But that day he looked disheveled, disoriented, not like the guy who'd wooed me and who I'd fallen for two years earlier.

A few months after the last time, I heard the police found his body dumped somewhere along Highway 1 outside San Francisco. He died of an overdose of heroin. Though he deserved the dog bite, he didn't deserve to die like that.

The last time I saw him was in a dream not long ago. He was smiling, easygoing, elusive, just as he'd been in life. We were on an icy mountaintop in a glass-enclosed room with a view of the snow outside. He sat at a table strewn with gleaming gems of all hues, perhaps symbolic of how attached he'd been to earthly wealth. Despite what had happened between us in life, I was again drawn to him as we spoke.

When the time arrived for yet one more separation, he told me to call him. Part of me still wanted to, and yet this time I knew I wouldn't.

Contributors' Notes

J.D. Blackrose works in corporate communications and lives with her husband, three children, and an enormous orange cat. She's fearful that so-called normal people will discover exactly how often she thinks about wicked fairies, nasty wizards, homicidal elevators, treacherous forests, and the odd murder, even when she is supposed to be having coffee with a friend or cheering her daughter on during a soccer game. As a survival tactic, she has mastered the art of looking interested.

Herta B. Feely's novel, *Saving Phoebe Murrow*, was released this fall in print and e-book form by Upper Hand Press in the U.S. and Twenty7 Books in the U.K. She has been awarded the James Jones First Novel Fellowship, an Artist Fellowship in Literature from the D.C. Commission on the Arts and Humanities, and the American Independent Writers' award for best personal essay in 2010. She is also a reviewer for the Washington Independent Review of Books and owner of Chrysalis Editorial, which serves writers in a variety of capacities—from evaluating manuscripts to ghostwriting to working as a writing coach. www.chrysaliseditorial.com and www.hertafeely.com

Dakota James is originally from Texas and now lives in Brooklyn, N.Y. His short stories have been published in Pilcrow & Dagger, Scarborough Fair Magazine, the Saturday Evening Post, and Headland. James is also the personal assistant and devoted errand-boy to playwright and novelist Theresa Rebeck.

Troy D. Kurz is a writer of horror, dark fantasy, and weird fiction tales. He lives in the Fredericksburg, Va., area and is at work on many other stories with the help of his girlfriend and personal editor Shannon Christopher.

Meredith Maslich is originally from Rochester, N.Y., and now lives in the suburbs of Washington, D.C. When she isn't running Possibilities Publishing Company and its subsidiaries Sparkle&Snark and Thumbkin Prints, she's a storytelling teacher and corporate trainer for Story District. She is also a recipient of an esteemed Fabby Award for Outstanding Contributions to Storytelling.

Joani Peacock is an Episcopal priest and associate for "Liturgy & Hilarity" at Emmanuel on High in Alexandria, Va. She is also a blogger, storyteller, and mental health evangelist @Unorthodox & Unhinged and @Sex & The Single Vicar. In addition, she is a cheerleader for and veteran of the Story District stage; bibliomaniac volunteer at the Library of Congress; Washington, D.C., born and bred; half-marathoner and avid pedestrian; friend to many and mother of three.

Jim Ryan is from Avon, N.Y.—home to countless stars, cows, and old pickups. When he isn't writing or working, he enjoys fishing, playing games, and making or listening to music. He is a graduate of SUNY Geneseo's creative writing program, where he helped found and later contributed to the literary journal Gandy Dancer. His stories "How to Walk in the Dark" and "Window Seat" can be found there.

Other Books by Possibilities Publishing Company

NOVELS

Unfit: A Novel
by Lara Cleveland Torgesen

Becoming Jonika
by PJ Devlin

The Plan
by Samantha Powers

The Pursuit
by Samantha Powers

Wishes, Sins and the Wissahickon Creek
by PJ Devlin

Wissahickon Souls **(Book Excellence Award Finalist)**
by PJ Devlin

ANTHOLOGIES

Sucker for Love: *True Tales about Loves Lost, Found and Imagined*

Trick or Treat! *A Collection of Spooky Stories*

Besties, Bromances & Soulmates: *Stories about Pivotal Relationships*

NON-FICTION

Sell More Easily
by Howard Maslich

Your Genius Within
by Victor Garlock

Freak Show Without a Tent
by Nevin Martell

Crocodile Charlie and the Holy Grail
by John Kolm and Peter Ring

37212357R00033

Made in the USA
Middletown, DE
22 November 2016